T5-AFS-904

HELLO!

by Alma Flor Ada   illustrated by Garin Baker

Harcourt

Orlando   Boston   Dallas   Chicago   San Diego

Visit *The Learning Site!*

www.harcourtschool.com

When I arrived here, I didn't know what *hello* and *good-bye* meant. Now I say *hello* to greet people I see every day.

"Hello, Mrs. Park!"

"Hello, Ana!"

I say *good-bye* when I won't see someone for a while.

"Good-bye, Grandma. I'll miss you!"

When I arrived here, I didn't know what *good morning* and *good night* meant. Now I say *good morning* to my family at breakfast time.

"Good morning, Mami. I smell toast and eggs. They smell delicious!"

4

I say *good night* to my father when he tucks me into bed.

"Good night, Papi. I'm very sleepy."

When I arrived here, I didn't know what *please* and *thank you* meant. Now I say, "Please pass the butter, Carmen."

After Carmen gives me the butter, I say, "Thank you!"

Carmen says, "You're welcome."
That is what you say to someone after
they have thanked you for something.

When I arrived here, someone asked me, "How are you?" I didn't know what she meant. Now I ask my friends, "How are you?" I want to know if they are feeling fine or not so good.

When someone asks me, "How are you, Ana?" I say, "I'm fine, thank you." If I am not feeling very well, I might say, "I don't feel well, but thank you for asking."

When I arrived here, I didn't know what to say when I met someone new. Now I say, "It's nice to meet you." I like to meet new friends.

When I make new friends, I invite them to play with me. Sometimes I ask them if I may play with them. I say, "May I play soccer with you tomorrow?" I know it will be fun!

When I arrived here, I didn't know
what *excuse me* or *I'm sorry* meant.
Now I know that when I want
someone to move out of my way, I
should say, "Excuse me, please."

If I step on someone's toe, I feel bad about that. I say, "I'm sorry!" Most of the time, the other person says, "That's okay." Then we both smile.

When I arrived here, I didn't know what *Good luck!* meant. Now when my friend Tran is going to take a test, I say "Good luck!" I know Tran studied very hard for the test. I say *Good luck!* because I hope he gets an A!

When I arrived here, I didn't know what *Happy birthday!* meant. Now I say *Happy birthday!* to my family and my friends on their birthdays. On August 1, I said, "Happy Birthday, Rosita!" On November 4, I said, "Happy Birthday, Philip!"

On May 27, everyone said to me, "SURPRISE!"